Landon RIDES THE SUBWAY

written by Diana Perez

Henry &
Miles !
Enjoy the
ride !

DPerez

Love
Landon

For my son, Landon.
May you never fear this world, and explore it for all its beauty.

ISBN 978-1-941434-85-7 Text copyright© 2017 by StoryBook Genius Publishing, LLC.
Illustrations copyright©2017 by StoryBook Genius Publishing. All rights reserved.

STORYBOOK
GENIUS PUBLISHING
sbgpublishing.com

yip jar Book Design by yipjar.com

Today was an

exciting day!

The sun was shining,

the birds were

chirping and

Landon's mom

had promised to

take him to the museum!

He had heard so much about the museum.

Big dinosaur bones,

a room full of butterflies,

and a giant whale hanging off the ceiling.

He hurried and got dressed
extra quickly today.

Not only were they going to the museum...

they were going to ride the subway!

Landon held

his mom's hand

as they hurried down

the long stairs.

Under the big city he loves so much,

Landon heard music playing.

He saw people dancing, and there was even a clown!

What a great place this was! It was a whole new world.

Mom looked for the right sign
and found the way to the

train.

Exit

79 Street
Museum of Natural History
Uptown & Bronx   B C

The train was roaring
through the tunnel so fast.
Landon could see
the train lights getting closer.

The train was here!

Exit

B

The doors opened and everyone
walked onto the train.

The doors closed and off they went

to the museum

...Landon and his mom.

Landon looked
all around the train.

It was

magical!

All of a sudden,
a man started singing!

It was a beautiful song.
Landon had heard this song before.

It was a song from one of his favorite movies!

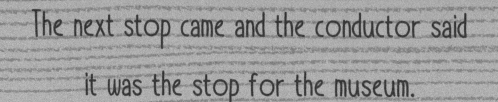
The next stop came and the conductor said

it was the stop for the museum.

Landon and his mom got off the train...

81ST ST. MUSEUM OF
NATURAL H

The man behind the counter handed
Landon his ticket to the museum.

"Wow...look at those dinosaurs!" said Landon.

The museum was more amazing than Landon had imagined!

CPSIA information can be obtained
at www.ICGtesting.com
Printed in the USA
BVHW02*2351211018
530274BV00004BA/10/P

9 781941 434857